Vegas Mistake

Mylia Ashton

Published by Colors of Love, 2015.

---

1.   https://subscribeto.eo.page/myliaashton

Table of Contents

Author's Note

THE EBOOK VERSION OF this book is free for newsletter subscribers. To offer it as a print book, it has to be a minimum number of pages, so I'm including excerpts so readers who prefer print can still obtain this book. Thanks!

Vegas Mistake
Mylia Ashton

Blurb

Best night ever or biggest mistake of her life?
WHILE AT THE VENETIAN for her best friend's whirlwind wedding, curvy Justina decides to cut loose and have a one-night stand for the first time in her thirty-four years. Handsome Michael is perfect and drawn to her curves. Their sweet, passionate night leaves both longing for more, but will Justina discover she's made a giant Vegas mistake?

This is a BWWM romance with a touch of steam, mistaken identities, and a dash of fairytale.

Chapter One

JUSTINA UNDERHILL LED her inebriated friend back to the hotel room Elena had reserved at the Venetian on the Strip. It was quite a feat to get her to the eighth-floor room, because both women had imbibed more than a few martinis at Elena's bridal shower held in the V Bar downstairs.

"I love you, Justina," said Elena, giving her an exuberant hug that nearly knocked them both off balance. The petite bride-to-be tottered in her four-inch heels, but steadied herself against Justina.

"I love you too." She was slightly more sober than her friend and managed to steer them to the right room. After all, it was her duty as maid-of-honor to make sure her friend survived until the wedding. That prevented her from drinking as freely.

"I love Mitchell so much." She threw her arms wide, nearly taking a dive in the process. "I just love the whole world."

Justina managed to catch her, supporting her tiny friend with her bigger frame. Next to Elena, most women seemed large, but she seemed huge in comparison. Most days, she tried not to draw comparisons between them, but tonight, vulnerable from the alcohol and her own envy of Elena's happiness, it was impossible to not come up wanting. Miss Petite versus Miss Curvy? Of course she would feel inadequate.

She pushed Elena gently against the wall so she could search for the keycards to their rooms in the impractical black bag she carried. It matched the plunging, sequined dress perfectly, but had just enough space for a credit card, her ID, two keycards, and a lipstick.

"You deserve to be as happy as I am." Elena rubbed her face against the wall, as if snuggling the elegantly striped gold and taupe wallpaper.

"I agree."

"Someday, you'll meet the right man...he won't care about anything but who you are."

Elena's comment sobered her up slightly. Justina retrieved her friend's keycard and slid it through the reader on the first try. She put an arm around Elena's waist to guide her into the luxurious room and dumped her a little less than gently onto the bed. Normally, her friend wouldn't have broached the topic of her weight, and Justina would never bring it up on her own. "I'm going to my room now. Call me if you need anything."

Without bothering to strip out of the slinky black and silver skirt or red velvet tank top that were such a striking contrast to her ebony skin, she kicked off her heels, curled up with the pillow, and asked, "Whoever decided I couldn't see Mitchell before the wedding? It's a stupid tradition."

"It's not the just the tradition, remember? His flight didn't arrive from the UK until this afternoon." Her white fiancé had spent the last six months working in England, learning the banking industry. He had another six months of his assignment ahead of him, but the two lovers had decided they couldn't wait any longer to get married and had thrown together the upcoming ceremony in two weeks. "By the time he made it to his bachelor party, he wouldn't have had time to come see you tonight." She pushed the hair off Elena's face. "You'll see him tomorrow afternoon in the chapel."

"'Going to the chapel...'" Elena mumbled the rest of the lyrics into her pillow, if she continued singing. That was one area where Justina had no reason to envy her friend. She sounded like someone torturing a bullfrog whenever she burst into song.

"Good night, Elena."

"'Night, Justina." Almost immediately, her loud snores filled the room.

Justina left her friend after covering her with a blanket. As she walked out of the suite, headed to her own room, she decided she wasn't yet ready to retire. It was almost three a.m., but the pleasant buzz she'd been riding the past few hours had mostly dissipated, and she wanted it back. After all, she was young, single, and in Sin City. It would be criminal not to take advantage of all the delights Vegas had to offer.

Besides, it had been way too long since she'd gotten laid. She might not find a partner, but she could at least test the waters.

JUSTINA WALKED INTO the Tao Nightclub a few minutes later. The last thing she wanted to do was put a damper on the men's fun. She scanned the room as quickly as she could, looking for remnants of Mitchell's bachelor party. Though she had never met the groom, she knew several of the men who would have attended, including Elena's two brothers and cousins. No one looked familiar, so she slipped into a free seat on one of the upholstered benches. Two men were a couple of cushions away, and she considered making eye contact and trying to strike up a conversation. Her core quivered when she imagined what it would be like to have two lovers at one time.

The passionate kiss the men leaned forward to exchange soon broke up that fantasy. With a sigh, Justina forced herself to look away from the strangely arousing display, not wanting to be a peeping Tom.

As she glanced across the room, her gaze collided with a set of piercing green eyes. They seemed to hold her spellbound, and she couldn't break free from his stare. As the white man the eyes belonged to raised his glass to her, she smiled a bit uncertainly in return. He seemed tall, even seated, with wavy brown hair, a nice tan, and smooth, handsome features. His body looked lean and honed under the dark suit. That man could have his pick of any woman in the place—and there were several hotties still partying—so it seemed unbelievable that he could really be flirting with her.

She tried to dismiss the moment and let her gaze slide away. What she had deemed flirting might not be anything more than drunken friendliness on his part. It was just one of the many frustrating things about men. Justina had no idea how to properly read their signals.

A server approached, and she ordered a Cosmo from the tall, skinny woman. After she'd left, Justina continued to look around the room, suddenly feeling out of place. The largest woman might have been a size-six. The go-go dancers were probably in the negative sizes. It wasn't a place for a woman who preferred Ben & Jerry's to Jenny Craig.

Justina attempted to shake herself out of her funk in the few minutes it took for her waitress to return with the drink. She knew she was being too hard on herself. Most days, she was just fine with her curves, but Elena's impromptu wedding had put her in a self-pitying state that was annoying even herself.

"Don't be such an idiot," she said aloud, but softly. "I am a beautiful and special woman." The litany felt ridiculous on her tongue and had never worked. It had originated with the fifth counselor her stepmother had taken her to as a teen in order to help her find the emotional roots of her excess weight. Justina could say it all she wanted, but believing it was another story.

Casually, she completed a circuit of the room, slowly letting her gaze return to the spot where she had exchanged glances with that hot man. Her tummy dipped with disappointment when she saw he had gone. So much for that imagined interplay.

"Is this seat taken?"

With a blink, Justina jerked her gaze upward. It took every ounce of control not to let her mouth gape open when she saw the man from across the room now standing in front of her. He was taller than she had guessed, but just as athletic and sexy up-close. Reflexively, she looked to her left and right to make sure he wasn't talking to someone else standing behind her. Slowly, she nodded.

"It is?" He frowned, looking genuinely disappointed. "My apologies."

As he started to walk away, Justina found her voice. "Um, wait...the seat is free."

He turned around and took the spot beside her as though none of the awkwardness had occurred. When he held out his hand, the flash of gold drew her eyes to the Rolex just peeking out from the cuff of his white shirt. She took the hand automatically, nearly jumping out of her seat at the sparks that arced between them when his palm touched hers.

"I'm Michael."

"Justina Underhill." She still couldn't quite believe he was sitting there, conjured as if by magic, and it took her a moment to remember to let go of his hand. Sternly, she tried to compose herself and stop acting like an awestruck teenage girl.

Michael grinned. "That is a beautiful name."

She blushed, glad her mocha skin hid the reaction. "Um, thanks."

"What brings you to Vegas?"

"A wedding," she said.

"Yours?" he asked with an arched brow before sipping the amber liquid from his crystal glass.

"Not hardly." She nearly died when an unladylike snort escaped her.

"I would guess you don't hold much esteem for the institution?"

"It's fine for some, I guess." Justina ruthlessly squashed the little-girl voice in her head that tried to remind her of all the years she'd spent planning a fantasy wedding that seemed unlikely to take place. Far better to be pragmatic about not getting married and embrace it. After all, with sixty-percent of marriages ending in divorce, what was the point?

"Neither do I. Having experienced it once was enough for me."

She nodded. "Why are you here?"

Michael's luscious-looking lips bowed into a rueful smile. "For a wedding—not my own," he added with a sparkle in his eye.

Justina glanced at his left hand, finding it bare of a ring. "Divorced?"

"Yes." Michael seemed to lean in closer than necessary when he put his empty glass on the long table in front of the couch. "You?" His breath washed across her cheek, and he made no effort to move back.

"Not even close."

"Smart woman."

The conversation stuttered for a moment, and Justina cast about for something witty to say. Her brain seemed to be made of slush, and she cursed the number of drinks she'd had. If ever there was a time to be clearheaded, now was it. "Would you like to dance?" Her eyes widened when she issued the invitation. What the hell was she thinking? She hadn't danced in a long time.

"Yes." He took her hand, not giving her a chance to retract the invitation. Justina tried to convince herself all would be well. Michael already knew she was bigger than the stick women in the club. He'd have to be blind not to notice the discrepancy. The fact that he'd approached her had to mean something. Pressing her body against his probably wouldn't send him running away.

To her surprise, he bypassed the dance floor and led her up the staircase. As they neared the opened door of the balcony, the cool desert wind beckoned, blowing against her flushed face in a welcoming caress. She followed him outside, averting her eyes politely from the couples in various clenches congregated around the balcony. Few eyes focused on the gorgeous view of Vegas.

The music was still audible, but muted, allowing for conversation. Michael didn't seem to want to talk as he took her into his arms. Justina held herself stiffly, trying to keep her large breasts and her stomach from resting against his frame. When he started massaging the small of her back, she found it impossible to maintain her stiffness. With a small whimper of defeat, she melted against him.

"That's much better," he said through the thick fall of chemically relaxed hair covering her ear.

"It's a lovely night." The inane observation was silly, especially considering her view was basically the cut of his dark suit. At five-nine, she was tall, but he made her feel almost petite.

"Much lovelier now." The hand he'd had on her lower back inched downward. He paused at the curve of her hip, as if waiting to see if she would stop him.

Justina held her breath, indecision making the choice for her. When she didn't speak up or step away, Michael rested his hand on her buttocks, squeezing lightly. She shivered at the contact.

"Cold?" The huskiness in his tone revealed his own excitement.

"Hot," she said brazenly.

Michael pulled her closer, moving both hands to massage her ass. "I couldn't agree more."

Justina swore she had to be dreaming as Michael eased her against the wall, somewhat in shadows. He kept a hand possessively on her right butt cheek, but brought the other one around to rest just under her breast. She tipped back her head as he lowered his, parting her lips in invitation. His mouth was firm and sure against hers, his lips forming to hers as though they had been molded to fit together. She sighed into his mouth, overwhelmed by how perfect the kiss was.

Michael slipped his tongue inside, stroking hers in a languorous fashion. Justina darted her tongue around his, parrying and thrusting with lustful intensity. When he lifted his head, she whimpered at the lost contact.

He cupped her breast, his thumb stroking a circle just outside the boundary of her nipple. "I'd like to say something, but I don't know whether to be blunt, or if I should tiptoe around it for a bit first."

Instinctively, Justina tensed, preparing herself for a commentary on her body. It wouldn't be the first time a man had said something cruel in the heat of the moment, perhaps thinking he was doing her a favor by pointing out her flaws—as though she remained unaware of them. "I prefer honesty," she said coolly, already mentally disengaging from the handsome stranger who still held her so intimately.

"I want to have sex with you."

Chapter Two

HER EYES WIDENED, AND she blinked. "What?" It wasn't outside the realm of possibility, especially considering the proof of arousal pressed against her stomach, but when she had been preparing herself for rejection, she couldn't quite wrap her mind around what he was saying so candidly. "I think I misheard."

A slow, sexy grin curved his lips upward. "No, you didn't. I want to take you up to your room—or mine—and strip off that dress. When I see what's underneath, I want to take it off too." He dipped his head to bring his mouth closer to her ear as a couple wandered by them. "My hands are aching to hold your luscious breasts, and my cock is twitching just thinking about how it will feel to be inside your hot, wet heat."

Justina's mouth was dry as the desert surrounding the oasis that was Las Vegas. She longed for something to drink. More than that, she longed to make his words a reality. "All right."

He brushed his lips against her cheek. "I didn't frighten you away with my frankness?"

She tipped her head back to meet his gaze. "Not at all. It's refreshing."

As Michael curved his arm around her waist, Justina fell into step with him, moving in harmonious rhythm as they reentered the club and walked through it, dodging people at every turn. "I think it's either all the whiskey I drank at the bachelor party, or maybe it's just this place. Whatever the reason, I'm not usually so brash back home in Boston."

"That's a pity." Justina didn't admit she wasn't either. Never in thirty-four years had she indulged in a one-night stand. It was about time she did, and what better place than here, with the perfect partner? "It might work every time."

They stopped to wait for the elevator, sharing the space with a couple embracing passionately. "I'm just happy it worked tonight."

"So am I." As they stepped onto the elevator, she fished inside her dinky purse for the keycard to her room. "I'm on eight."

"Ten." He shrugged. "You're closer."

By mutual agreement, they reached for the eight button at the same time. Justina's body hummed with anticipation as the lift whisked them higher. Michael maintained a slight distance between them until the fourth floor, where they lost their riding companions. As soon as the doors closed behind them, he pressed his body against hers, his erection pushing insistently into her lower back. With one big hand, he cupped her breast, squeezing the soft globe gently. "I can't wait to get you out of these clothes."

"I'm looking forward to it." She was excited about the coming encounter, but nausea churned in her stomach. It would be a new experience to bare her body to a man she didn't know. The handful of lovers she'd had previously had all been friends first, and their relationships had been well established before getting physical. Justina had always given the men in her life ample opportunity to be on familiar terms with her first, so that if they found the outside disappointing, at least they would know the person she was. It had been her way of compensating. With Michael, he would be accepting or rejecting her strictly on the basis of her physical form. The prospect was daunting.

At her room, she slid in the keycard and preceded him inside. Justina tossed her purse on the ornate table by the door and turned on the light for the entryway. The sleeping area remained shrouded in shadows.

She turned to him, cocking her head. "Since we're being blunt, do you have protection?"

Michael patted his pocket. "Sure do."

Relaxing marginally, she kicked off the stunning black heels that had been killing her feet half the night. Suddenly nervous, she walked to the phone. "Shall I call for something? Champagne?"

He shook his head, following her. Justina tried to hide her anxiety behind boldness. With sure hands, she stripped away his suit jacket as soon as he came into range. Simultaneously, she stretched upward to capture his lips for a deep kiss. Now three inches shorter without the heels, he really did tower over her.

With expertise she didn't know she had, Justina licked and teased his mouth and lips, alternately sucking on his tongue before nipping him. She kept her hands moving ceaselessly, first working at the knot precariously holding his crooked tie, and then assigning her fingers the task of unbuttoning his shirt.

His cufflinks proved a challenge, forcing Justina to break the kiss. She lowered her mouth to his chest, running her tongue across his skin in random patterns. Without looking down, she managed to undo each cufflink and button. Feeling an unreasoning sense of accomplishment, she dropped the shirt onto the floor and stretched to place the cufflinks on the dresser.

"You move fast, Justina."

She smiled, looking up at him coyly through the fall of her lashes. "Sometimes...when I know what I want."

Michael chuckled, though he sounded strained. A flush to his cheeks betrayed the state she had worked him into, and she knew her face must reflect the same level of arousal. Unable to stop herself, she took a step closer, grasping the hair on his chest with her hands. Lightly, she scratched her manicured nails over one of his nipples, smiling with satisfaction at his harsh inhalation.

Justina dipped her head to soothe the raw flesh with her tongue. Michael tangled his hands into her elaborate coif, discarding pins with haste. She nipped his nipple in retaliation when he tugged her hair too hard.

"God, baby, do that again."

She arched a brow, amused that he found the act arousing. Gently, she bit him again, and then gasped when he tangled his hand in her loose hair, pushing her face tighter against his chest.

"Harder."

Justina sucked the nipple and surrounding flesh into her mouth, biting down on the bud with as much force as she dared. Michael cried out, but she didn't stop. There had been only a tiny measure of pain in the cry, but far more enjoyment. She stopped biting for a moment to tease the nipple, stroking gently with her tongue. As she nurtured that one, she raked her nails across his neglected nipple, enjoying the way his body trembled. When she bit him again, Michael cried out her name in what sounded more like a hoarse grunt than a word.

Bolstered by his response, she moved her hands to his waistband, undoing the leather belt quickly. Her fingers were nimble over the zipper and button of his trousers, and she stripped them to his feet in seconds. Before continuing, Justina took a step back. It seemed like her fingers stumbled over the simple process of undoing the button on her dress, but the zipper slid down easily. She stepped out of it, feeling self-conscious of her voluptuousness. Michael drew in a deep breath, but she didn't wait to find out if it was one of appreciation or disappointment.

Dropping to her knees, she brought a hand up to his black briefs. He pulsed visibly through the fabric, and she couldn't resist stroking the length of him. "I can't wait to taste you." She looked up at him from her subservient position, licking her lips. Michael had tossed back his head and seemed on the verge of losing control. Justina squeezed the head, grazing the tip with her nails.

"Justina...let me..." He broke off as she lowered his briefs to meet his pants. "Seriously, I want to give you some attention."

"You'll have your opportunity." Not giving him a chance to lodge any more protests, Justina put her mouth around his shaft. She inhaled deeply, suctioning air around the head. He jerked in response, and she repeated the action. Michael was stiff with tension and arousal, his entire body emitting waves of anticipation. Justina swirled her tongue around the corona, warming him up.

Michael put his hand against the back of her head, grasping a handful of her hair. "You're killing me."

"Just a little death." She breathed against his skin with each word, enjoying the way his body twitched. Justina slid her mouth down the shaft, relaxing her throat as his head reached the back of her mouth. His pre-ejaculate streamed into her mouth, and she savored the salty tang as she lavished attention on his aroused length.

"I'm about to come."

In response, she increased suction, crying out with surprise when Michael jerked away from her. Justina sat back on her heels, staring up at him with confusion and a touch of hurt. He twisted partially from her with his shoulders slumped. His ragged inhalations filled the room, and it took him several moments before he turned back to her.

Justina almost recoiled when he brushed his hand against her cheek.

"I'm sorry. I just didn't want it to be that way. I want to be inside you." The red stain on his cheeks seemed to come from embarrassment rather than exertion. "You make me feel like a horny teenager all over again. Only problem is, I'm afraid my hair trigger won't reset as fast as it did back then, and you deserve better than that."

Charmed by the admission, Justina smiled. She rubbed her cheek against his hand, and then rose to her feet. "How do you want it to be?"

"Me inside you." He reached for her, putting his arms around her. Without a trace of hesitation, Michael captured her mouth for a kiss, plunging his tongue inside her moist depths. Justina returned it enthusiastically. She ached with the need for release and shifted impatiently.

Apparently, Michael wouldn't be rushed. He released her mouth and paused to take off his shoes, socks, and pants. Then he stared at her corset with a look of deep concentration. "How do you get this thing off?"

"There's a button under the collar." Justina showed him. When she started to undo the cleverly hidden closure that kept the strip of satin around her torso, he pushed away her hand.

"My turn to do the undressing," he said for an explanation. His hands, seemingly more suited to a task like building a house, had no trouble with the delicate button. Once he had dispensed with that, Michael found the zipper at the side and divested her of the garment.

She shivered, stomach clenched with dread, as she stood before him in the plunging velvet bra, matching lace and velvet panties, and black pantyhose. Justina hated to reveal herself so vividly. When he walked over to turn on the lamp by the bedside, the light made her vulnerability all the worse. She followed quickly, reaching to turn off the light he'd just turned on. Michael intercepted her hand with a frown of confusion. "I like it dim. It's...cozier." It sounded lame even to her ears, and she could tell he didn't believe her.

Michael pulled her away from the lamp, leaving it on. "I want to see you. Every last inch."

It should have been sexy, but the words just increased her anxiety. She always made love with the lights out. Until Michael, no man had ever countered her unspoken edict.

Torn between fear and excitement, Justina tried to remain relaxed as Michael undid the clasp of her bra. The velvet underwire style opened, spilling forth her large breasts. With more haste than finesse, he tossed the undergarment aside and reached forward like a little boy eager to get his hands on sweets. She gasped when he took her breasts in his hands, pushing them together as he massaged the tender tissue.

"They're perfect, Justina. Big, glorious, and tipped with the most perfect brown buds." Michael dipped his head to flick his tongue across one. "I could spend hours just feasting on your breasts."

A film of perspiration broke out on her body as he guided her back to the bed. Justina sprawled across it, pushing aside worries of her appearance as he positioned his body above hers, his mouth at her breast.

While he suckled one nipple, he paid equal attention to her other breast. His fingers worked magic on her skin, stroking, tugging, and coaxing the bud to a hardened state she had never attained.

Eventually, Michael seemed to have gotten enough of her breasts, at least temporarily. He withdrew from her, and Justina turned to lie on her side so she could see what he was doing. She watched him walk to his clothes and search in his pants. When he walked back to her with a small strip of condoms, her thighs quivered with anticipation. She patted the bed when he stood above her without moving.

"You are really incredible, Justina." He tossed the condoms on the soft coverlet before bending over her. She caught her breath when he pulled down her pantyhose, lifting each leg to help him remove the thin silk. She couldn't help arching her hips upward as he stroked her through the crotch. Michael seemed to delight in his unhurried tactile exploration of the lace pattern, spending an inordinate amount of time running his thumb along the seam where lace met the velvet panel above her mound. She cried out when he pressed his thumb into the center of her slit, finding her clit unerringly. "So incredible."

Justina writhed impatiently. "Please, Michael."

With a chuckle, he stripped her of the panties. Justina held her breath when he caressed the outside of her pussy with two of his fingers. She arched her hips to take the digits inside when he neared her opening. He evaded the maneuver by sliding his fingers north, once again seeking out her clit. She gasped when he circled the aching bud with his forefinger, and then gasped again when he abruptly dipped his thumb inside. She watched through heavy eyes as he brought it to his mouth to lick off her essence.

"Mmm." He closed his eyes for a moment, as if savoring the taste. When the lids fluttered open, his eyes seemed like smoldering emeralds. "You're wet and ready, aren't you, baby?"

"I've been ready since our eyes met."

Michael laughed, but it was a strained sound that betrayed how much his apparent control was costing him. "If I'd had my way, I would have walked over to you, pinned you to that couch, and fucked you senseless in front of everyone."

An intense jolt of pleasure shot through her as her mind supplied a visual to accompany his words. She giggled, imagining the shocked onlookers. If the bookmakers took the bet, she'd lay odds that not one of them would have looked away from such a startling sight as two people fucking in the middle of a trendy club.

In seconds, Michael had torn open the condom and slid it on. Justina parted her thighs as he knelt between them. A last-minute dart of doubt tried to pierce the euphoric haze surrounding her, but she successfully quashed it. Maybe all the years she'd spent working on her self-image were finally paying off.

Or maybe Michael had made her so hot she couldn't think straight. It was a heady feeling.

Not as heady as having him surge inside her. Her body fell into the age-old rhythm, following the pace he set. Michael seemed to know instinctively when to vary his speed, or rotate his hips slightly to give her more stimulation. As she neared climax, he pushed her over the edge by bringing a hand between their bodies to squeeze her clit.

With a shout of satisfaction, she convulsed around him. Her orgasm must have triggered his, because he twitched inside of her several times, at first frenetically, and then gradually slowing.

When it was over, they lay together, their harsh breathing slowing to normal. Justina put her arms around Michael, content in a way she hadn't ever been before. She had no idea what time it was and didn't care. Even knowing he would probably leave sometime during the night, and she would never see him again couldn't totally spoil the blissful aftermath.

Sleep stole over her, and she tried to fight it, not wanting to relinquish the night with Michael just yet. Satisfaction and physical exhaustion, coupled with the unaccustomed amount of alcohol she had imbibed, combined to undo her resolve, and her eyes closed. She was aware of slipping into slumber, but powerless to fight it.

Chapter Three

MICHAEL WOKE SOMETIME later, still holding Justina. She snored softly, oblivious to everything. Staring down at her beautiful face, his cock swelled with renewed arousal. A man driven by his senses, her perfection nearly overwhelmed him. Soft and smooth everywhere, with generous curves and a womanly frame, he could spend years getting acquainted with her body and never grow tired of it.

It killed him that she didn't see how beautiful she was. Justina had made every effort to hide her self-consciousness, but he'd seen through her façade. Everything she'd done, from turning the focus on him, to trying to put out the lights, had screamed that she wanted to hide from him. Michael was thrilled she had wanted him enough to get past her issues, but he yearned to show her just how sexy she was.

He stroked his fingers lightly across her stomach, smiling when she twitched in her sleep. He traced a circle around her belly button, and she grunted. When Michael moved his fingers up to her breast, lightly trailing his forefinger around her nipple, she made an undecipherable noise and turned over from her side to her stomach.

Undeterred by her remaining asleep, he shifted positions so he could lean over her. She jumped when he wafted a breath of hot air across her skin. Michael blew again, concentrating on her lower back. Justina tensed when he grazed her spine with his lips, but didn't appear to wake. He ran his tongue across her lower back and down the cleft of her buttocks. Her harsh inhalation broke the silence, indicating he had succeeded in rousing her. One goal accomplished, he turned to the next, which was to arouse her.

As her tension eased, he drew circles on her back, while moving his tongue lower. He chuckled again when she thrust her bottom into the air, giving him better access to her folds. She was sweet, yet tangy, on his tongue, and he lapped greedily. She squirmed, moaning each time he darted a tongue in and out of her opening.

When he stretched his tongue higher, seeking out her clit, she thrust back to meet him. Michael circled his tongue around the tight bud, enjoying her soft sighs. Unable to resist her heady flavor, he plunged his tongue into her again, thrusting in and out of her in mimicry of the way he wanted to drive his cock inside her.

She rolled onto her back, and Michael barely broke rhythm. Once she had settled, legs splayed, he grasped her soft thighs, kneading them as he sucked on. Justina arched off the bed, her hands balled around handfuls of the coverlet. Her obvious pleasure fed his own, and he had to mentally count to ten to keep from blowing everything by driving into her wet heat then and there.

Diligently, Michael licked her until she bucked her hips against his hand and face, guttural groans falling from her lips. He let out a cry of his own when she squeezed her thighs tightly around his head. Her sheath convulsed around his fingers, and she whimpered, seemingly too out of breath to manage anything more taxing.

Michael didn't give her a chance to compose herself or withdraw back into her shell. Tongue extended, he licked a trail from her neatly trimmed curls to her left breast. He fastened his lips around the globe, sucking the nipple and part of the areola inside his mouth. While flicking his tongue across the hard bead, he thrust his fingers in and out of her pussy at a slow pace. His intent wasn't to make her come again—yet—but just to keep her stimulated.

"What are you doing to me, Michael?" she asked hoarsely.

He lifted his mouth from her breast to look into her eyes. "I'm seducing you, baby."

Justina blinked. "You've already had me."

"Not the right way." He lowered his head again, once more taking a generous mouthful of her breast, this time focusing his attention on the right one. Simultaneously, he wriggled his fingers inside her, probing as deeply as he could.

"What's that mean?" She let out a startled yelp, indicating he had found a particularly sensitive spot.

Ignoring her question, he raked his teeth across her nipple, pleased when she arched her back. Michael swept his tongue around the hard pearl, finding her tastier than any ice cream. He had started out with the intent of seducing her senses, but that didn't mean he couldn't enjoy his work. He ached, pulsing in time with the contractions around his finger as her body strove for orgasm.

When she buried her fingers in his hair, Michael allowed her to pull his head up toward her mouth. He paused along the way to suck on her throat. She whimpered when he drew in a bit of flesh at the bend of her neck to nip it. Justina's creamy brown skin had a faint taste of perspiration as he ran his tongue from her throat to her mouth, where he spent long minutes licking each plump contour. Finally, he responded to the invitation she issued with her opened mouth and darted his tongue inside. Her unique taste got to him, making the blood rush through his head.

His thinking clouded by the intoxicating taste of her mouth, it took Michael a moment to realize she had pushed away the hand he'd had in her slit, wrapped her thighs around his hips, and was working on slipping a condom over his cock. Michael tensed, trying to resist. "No."

She arched a brow, finishing sheathing him in latex before asking, "Why not?"

Shaking his head, he pulled back from the wet heat trying to draw him in. "I want it to be special for you."

"It is, Michael." She clutched his biceps, and he couldn't keep resisting when she tightened her thighs to pull him closer. "This has been one of the best nights of my life. Please."

The request melted his resolve. His erection swelled, the head nestling into her opening. Michael sank inside her as she lifted her hips, and he couldn't remember how to breathe for a second. It had been only a few hours, but he had forgotten just how amazing she felt—hot, tight, and so wet he could thrust into her for hours.

Her soft body cushioned his, and he experienced renewed appreciation for her beauty. His friends had sometimes mocked his taste in women, but he pitied them for their ignorance. They would never know the delicious thrill of a voluptuous woman's embrace, of the softness of her skin, and the erotic sensation of generous curves that welcomed him.

Their pace was slow, as if time had no meaning. Michael lost himself in Justina's wide brown eyes, enthralled by the depth of pleasure reflected through her veil of thick, black lashes. "You have the most beautiful eyes." He smiled when her cheeks flushed. "They remind me of the trees turning in autumn at my parents' vacation home in Vermont."

She cleared her throat. "You don't have to work at seducing me anymore, hon."

He buried his face against the silkiness of her black hair, inhaling the fruity scent. Doing his best to memorize everything about the woman in his arms, he focused on all aspects of her. It was unlikely that he would ever see her again after tonight, and he wanted to remember Justina Underhill. She was an unforgettable woman.

Her breathless cries and convulsing womb signaled her release, allowing Michael to give in to the orgasm washing through him. His body shook under the onslaught, and he nearly lost the ability to hold himself up on his arms for a moment. He couldn't help whispering her name repeatedly as he spilled his seed inside her through the thin barrier of latex separating them.

How he longed to feel her clenching directly around his bare shaft, but it was too risky to do something like that with a one-night stand. If only he could see her again. But that was impossible. They were both in town for just a couple of days. He had no idea where she was from, or how far apart they lived. His own uncertainty kept him from suggesting any sort of serious relationship as they lay together in the sweet bliss of afterglow. Instead, he just held her, holding back the words his heart wanted him to utter.

Chapter Four

"JUSTINA!"

She jumped, focusing her eyes on Elena, whose expression revealed she had been trying to get her attention for quite some time. Heat suffused her face when she realized she had been daydreaming about last night. Even worse, she'd been dwelling on the note she'd awakened to, where Michael left his cell number and implied he wanted to see her again. She had been busy trying to work out the logistics of that. "Yes, what?"

"Do you know if the staff put out the right centerpieces? Yesterday, they had a hideous shade of orange mixed in with the white and coral flowers."

Justina picked up the hairbrush on the vanity and began smoothing the long fall of Elena's straightened dark hair trailing down her back from the elegant knot atop her head. "They hadn't finished setting up everything, but the centerpieces were out. They looked right when I checked out the ballroom before coming here to help you get ready."

"Thank goodness." Her shoulders, bared by the cut of the strapless princess dress, seemed to relax. "I tell you, I had no idea how stressful it would be to throw together a last-minute wedding like this. Maybe we should have waited until Mitchell finishes his internship and had the wedding in Boston like his mother wanted."

She shrugged, not looking up from smoothing the wrinkles from the back of Elena's dress. "It might have been practical, but you didn't want to wait for him, did you?"

"No." She let out a sigh that could have rivaled any schoolgirl's thinking of her crush. "He's so wonderful. I can't wait for you to meet him."

"I'd like that. All you've done is talk about him ever since you came back." Elena had met Mitchell while she was visiting her father, an expatriate living in London. Theirs had evidently been a whirlwind romance, and he had proposed before she flew back two weeks ago.

Justina emitted her own envious sigh, wishing something equally romantic could happen to her. For a moment, her mind conjured images of Michael, but she tried to ignore the thoughts. Last night had been wonderful, and if she were lucky, they might have another night or two together in Vegas, but she should resign herself to knowing that was all they could have.

"Did I tell you Mitchell's family flew in for the wedding? I thought his mother wouldn't come, because she was so angry that we were getting married like this, after only having known each other six weeks."

Justina patted Elena's shoulder, knowing how anxious she had been. "What changed her mind?"

She shrugged. "I guess Mitchell convinced her how in love we are." Elena turned her head away from the mirror to look up at Justina from her perch on the padded stool. "His parents are even letting us use their Vermont house for our honeymoon."

She froze, trying to sound casual, though alarm bells rang in her mind. "Where is Mitchell from again?"

Elena shook her head. "Honestly, you're not here today, are you? I must have said Boston a hundred times in the last few days. You should remember that I'm going back to London with Mitchell, but after his internship, we're settling in Boston."

On autopilot, she dropped the section of lace she'd been fluffing. "Excuse me. I have to check something."

"What?" Elena's mouth moved like a fish's out of water as Justina rushed past her. "Justina, what's wrong?" she called.

Justina kept going, headed straight for the ballroom reserved for the post-ceremony reception. They had still been setting up everything for the wedding when she had been in the Longhi room earlier to check the centerpieces. One of Elena's decorations included snapshots of her and Mitchell blown up to poster-size and mounted on the walls, to give their friends and family a sense of their courtship.

As she had expected, the staff, under the direction of the private coordinator Elena had hired, were in the process of mounting the last few pictures. Multiple images of the happy couple already adorned the walls, and Justina's stomach churned with nausea when she saw the smiling face of the future groom. He looked different with the petite Elena against a European backdrop than he had last night in her hotel room as he made love to her until she was limp, but she couldn't deny Mitchell was Michael.

She rushed from the ballroom, unable to stand the sight of Elena and Michael together. Anger and disgust thrummed through her. She had slept with her best friend's fiancé. God, how could Elena ever forgive her? It crossed her mind not to confess to her friend. If she could just keep it all to herself, Elena would never know.

The thought of keeping such an enormous secret had Justina falling against a wall, doubling over from pain in her chest. She couldn't do it. She couldn't let Elena blindly marry a man who would cheat on her the night before the wedding.

Blood rushed in her veins, and she was enraged with Michael, or Mitchell...or whatever he went by. Why hadn't she realized he was a sleaze? Elena had always been slightly naïve about people, but Justina seemed to have been born with natural cynicism. She always expected the worst to happen, so why had Michael blindsided her?

Still feeling sick, Justina stood up. She walked toward the rooms set aside for the wedding party to prepare before the ceremony scheduled to start in less than an hour at the Venetian Wedding Chapel. All too soon, her feet brought her to the brides' room, and she entered. To her relief, no one else was with Elena, who was absorbed in fiddling with her hair.

She looked up with a puzzled expression at her return. "Where did you rush off to, Justina?"

Justina walked over to her and knelt beside the stool, barely noticing the way the fabric of her dress tightened uncomfortably around her hips. "I had to check on something."

"Well, what?" asked her friend, exasperation evident.

"Your pictures in the ballroom."

Elena's eyes widened. "Oh, no. The studio screwed them up, didn't they? I knew better than to do it all online. I should have gone in person—"

She cut into Elena's panicked outburst. "They're fine." Justina bent her head. "God, I don't know how to tell you this." She felt even worse when Elena leaned forward to hug her.

"Whatever it is, I'm here for you. Just tell me."

Tears stung her eyes, and her voice was a rough croak when she blurted out, "I slept with a man I didn't know last night."

Elena blinked. "You?" She blinked again, sitting back. "Wow. That's not like you."

"I know."

She patted Justina's shoulder. "It will be all right. We all do stupid things, you know? I ended up in bed with Mitchell on our first date. I couldn't believe it was happening at the time, but I couldn't help myself."

So, the jerk always moved quickly. Anger reinforced her resolve, and she looked into Elena's eyes during her confession. "It was Mitchell. I didn't know it then, but I slept with your fiancé."

Elena seemed to wilt, her ebony skin taking on a grayish tinge. She bent over the vanity table. "What?" she asked in a whisper.

"I'm sorry." The tears broke past the dam that had held them in check, coursing down Justina's face. "I really didn't know. I never—"

Elena gained her feet abruptly, tossing her hairbrush at the mirror. The tinkle of glass was nothing compared to the loud shout her diminutive friend achieved. "How could you do that to me, Justina? How could you two go behind my back? You're my best friend." She scooped up a bottle of moisturizer from the assortment of cosmetics spread on the table, pitching it against the wall.

Justina cringed from Elena. Her anger was frightening, especially since Elena was usually collected and calm when faced with anything upsetting. She had never been one to throw things and scream. If not for the tears ruining her bridal makeup, she would have appeared just enraged. Justina knew her well enough to know Elena was only finding a physical outlet for her pain, because it was too great to hold inside.

She maintained her silence as Elena ranted, just standing back from the chaos. It wasn't until the door slammed against the wall and the groom came rushing through that she took her gaze from her friend. "You," she snarled as soon as she saw Mitchell rushing toward Elena.

"Elena, what's going on in here?" Mitchell reached his bride, pulling a compact from her hand. "What's wrong?"

Justina winced when Elena slapped Mitchell hard enough to have the sound reverberate throughout the room.

"You lying, cheating bastard."

Mitchell frowned. "What? Are you crazy, Elena?"

Elena jerked away from him. "How dare you sleep with my friend the night before our wedding?"

Reeling backward, Mitchell's eyes settled on Justina, and he seemed confused. "What...her?"

"Yes, her." Elena stamped her foot. "Why the pretense of wanting to settle down and raise a family if you were just going to sleep around?"

He shook his head. "Honey, I've never seen this woman before in my life, and I haven't been with any woman since I met you...and it was a long damn time before you that I last had a lover." Mitchell glared at Justina. "I don't know what your friend is trying to pull, but I never touched her."

"You liar." It was all Justina could do not to slap him herself. In the cold light of day, Michael was completely different. His face even looked harder, and his eyes, though green, weren't vibrant as they had been last night. How could she have found him so attractive before, when he left her cold now? It must be the harsh light of truth illuminating her thought processes.

Elena seemed torn. "Justina wouldn't lie."

"Neither would I," he said quietly, with so much sincerity that Justina almost believed him. He looked back at her again, still befuddled. "No offense, lady, but you aren't the type of girl I go for. You're more my..." He trailed off, a smile slowly forming on his face. "Wait right here."

"Where are you going?" Elena reached out to try to stop him from leaving, and Justina shook her head in amazement at his departure. Did he really think he could just walk out on the situation and leave it all for her and Elena to clean up?

Elena looked at Justina, her gaze searching. "You are telling me the truth, aren't you?"

Justina nodded, wishing she had been lying when she saw the agony in her friend's eyes.

The return of Mitchell interrupted their exchange, and he seemed excited. "I know what happened."

"So do I," said Justina. She wouldn't waver. It might be easier to pretend it had never happened, but Elena deserved a faithful husband.

As another man entered the room, Mitchell put an arm around his shoulders and dragged him forward. "Is this the guy you were with last night?"

Justina's mouth dropped open, and it took her a moment to comprehend her vision wasn't blurred. Twins! Dear god, they were nearly identical. In appearance, they were clones, though Michael's eyes were warmer, and his face more filled out. "Michael?"

"Justina?" He seemed confused. "What's going on? One minute, I'm squeezing into that darn tux, and the next Mitchell's telling me to get my butt into the brides' room."

Elena gasped, and it was a happy sound. She threw herself against Mitchell. "Oh, thank goodness."

Justina looked down, embarrassed and uncertain how to proceed. "I am so sorry, Elena...Mitchell. I had no idea you had a brother. A twin brother." To her relief, Elena let go of Mitchell to come over for a hug.

"It's okay. I should have mentioned Mitchell has a twin, but it just didn't occur to me." She withdrew, turning back to the two men. "You two clear out now and leave us to finish getting ready. And if you see the missing bridesmaids, send them in."

Mitchell was drawing Michael to the door, but his gaze hadn't left Justina's. "Seriously, what is going on?"

"Come on, bro, I'll tell you while we get dressed."

THE CELEBRANT NODDED to the bride and groom, who turned to face those assembled for the ceremony. "I present to you Mitchell and Elena Canard."

Justina wasn't sure if she or Michael clapped louder. Fortunately, he seemed to have taken the incident in stride and had even teased her about not being able to tell him apart from another man when they had reunited at the ceremony. She traded a glance with him from her side of the aisle, where she stood off to Elena's side. Her body hummed with anticipation while she waited for him to take her arm and lead her from the chapel as they followed the bride and groom.

They walked to the Longhi room together, arm in arm. Her bliss from the previous night had returned, lending everything a rosy air. She remained bubbly with optimism as they entered the room. Even when the throng of people separated them, she was bolstered each time she met Michael's gaze across the crowded room.

The first pinprick in her bubble of happiness appeared in the form of her stepmother. Justina's stomach churned with nausea when she almost walked right into the smaller woman. Ella took an exaggerated step back. "I know you're not very graceful, but please watch your step, dear."

That same tinkling laugh that had always followed her digs grated on Justina's nerves. She wanted to reply in a blithe manner, or even to just walk away from the woman who had made her teen years hell, but she couldn't seem to move her feet. Why did Ella always reduce her to this state?

What remained of her buoyant mood fled when the two stepsisters appeared on either side of Ella, completing the Trio of Evil, as she had dubbed them within days of meeting them. Sasha and Donella were beautiful young women with willowy frames and sleek dark hair that appeared to effortlessly fall in line with their commands—everything Justina wasn't.

She attempted to be polite, greeting the women. "What are you doing here?" she asked after the requisite exchange of pleasantries.

"I couldn't miss dear little Elena's wedding," said Ella. "She was over so often before you two left for college that I feel like she was one of my daughters."

Justina took a sip of champagne to hide her grimace. She knew Elena wouldn't have invited Ella or the stepsisters, so how had the other woman found out? "How did you hear of it?"

"Elena's mother. I ran into her at the spa. She invited me straightaway, as soon as she heard my invitation must have gotten lost." The flash in Ella's black eyes indicated she knew she had been shunned. Maybe that's why she had flown from Beverly Hills to Vegas. Her own perversity had driven her to the act.

"It's lovely to see you." Somehow, Justina managed to keep her tone civil. It was the same cool, distant voice she always used with Ella. They had never gotten along, but all pretense of a warm relationship had lapsed the day her father died. Even at his funeral, they had been cold with each other. Justina had only seen her stepmother a few times in intervening years, and each occasion was an ordeal.

"Speaking of weddings, did you get the card I sent to your little apartment in the Bronx?"

Justina nodded, ignoring the insult directed toward her apartment. It was actually a roomy two-bedroom, but Ella didn't believe any address outside of Manhattan could be anything but a hovel. "Congratulations are in order for you, Donella?"

Donella smiled, and somehow, it had the effect of making her seem even colder. "The wedding is late this year. I do hope you'll send a gift."

"Of course." She hid a dart of pain behind the fluted glass as she drained the last of the champagne. Why did these three still have the power to hurt her?

"I know you'll be much too busy to come."

"Yes. My job keeps me hopping."

"You're a secretary, aren't you?" asked Sasha with false sweetness.

"Assistant Director of IT for a major hospital, actually, but it's almost like being a secretary," she said with only a hint of mocking.

Ella looked her up and down. "I imagine it doesn't give you much time to get to the gym."

She looked away from Ella, in Donella's direction. "Is your fiancé here?"

"No, he had to attend a business meeting in Prague."

Justina nodded. "I'm sorry to hear that. It would have been nice to meet him." She began to look around the room, hoping to make eye contact with anyone in order to have an excuse to move on.

"My boyfriend is in the Bahamas, doing a photo shoot. He's representing one of the hottest designers of the year," said Sasha, her mouth curled into an unattractive sneer.

Justina was certain she disappointed her stepsister by not asking the name of the designer. "Well, if you'll excuse me, I should see if Elena needs anything." As she brushed past Ella, her stepmother caught her arm in a tight grip. She braced herself for whatever they wanted to say, praying they would get it over with quickly.

"Where is your date, dear Justina?" Ella smirked, and Donella actually giggled, as if the idea was laughable.

"Are you still with Penrod, that scientist you were dating for so long?" asked Sasha.

"Perry," she corrected with quiet dignity. "No, we haven't been together for some time." It had been three years since they'd split, so it must have been longer than that since she'd seen the Trio of Evil.

Ella clicked her tongue. "Let me offer you advice, Justina. You have to lose some weight. Start with gastric bypass. Afterward, I know a good plastic surgeon, who can do a tummy tuck, breast reduction, and rhinoplasty. Within a year, if you work at it, you could be passably pretty. Maybe it will be your wedding someday." She tilted her head. "If you keep up your unhealthy lifestyle, you'll never find a man."

Justina pursed her lips. She knew better than to argue, that the tirade would end faster if she maintained silence, but she couldn't resist the compulsion to speak. "Why do you care, Ella? We never see each other. I'm no longer around you to embarrass you with my appearance, so why are you still doing this?"

Ella blinked. "I promised your father I'd watch out for you."

She snorted. "Yeah, thanks." Justina started to walk past the three of them, but froze when her stepsisters giggled.

"I told you she wouldn't have a date," said Donella.

Sasha frowned. "Of course she doesn't, so don't make it sound like I was suggesting she would."

With a shake of her head, Justina took a couple of steps, moving from the Trio of Evil straight into Michael's arms. She looked up at him with a smile, feeling most of the sting of hurt dissipating under the calming light of his eyes. "I missed you," she whispered.

Ella managed to snatch her tentative happiness once more. Her trilling laugh caused Justina to stiffen her spine when her stepmother approached.

"My goodness, Justina, aren't you clumsy today?" She laughed again. "I did warn her to watch her step, but she has no grace. Mr....?"

Michael ignored the hand Ella extended in favor of shifting Justina to one arm. "Michael Canard."

"The groom's brother?" Sasha fluttered her eyelashes at him.

He nodded, and Justina held her breath, waiting to see if he would find Sasha and Donella as irresistible as every other man seemed to.

"Well, thank you for carrying familial duty above and beyond." Ella smiled in Justina's direction, but her glinting eyes held no warmth. "I'm so glad Justina has had someone to keep her company today."

"Oh, it was no problem." Michael put his hand on Justina's buttocks. "Being with Justina is a pleasure."

Donella arched a brow. "Really? I grew up with her, and I just can't imagine that."

Michael smiled as he squeezed her bottom tenderly. "Perhaps that's because you're a shallow bitch who wouldn't know a genuine person if they fell on you." He inclined his head to Ella. "It was enlightening meeting you, ma'am, but we must go. There are still pictures to take, and Elena has to throw the bouquet before I can steal Justina away and spend the night making love to her."

Justina's eyes widened, though not as much as The Trio of Evil's. She couldn't contain a startled laugh at their identical gasps of shock, and it turned to a giggle as Michael drew her away.

"Justina, you know those women aren't worth anything, don't you? Their opinion doesn't mean a damned thing," he said as he led her from the ballroom, to a private alcove set up for pictures.

She nodded. "My head knows it, but they still get to me."

He stopped in the hallway, turning her to face him. "You are beautiful, inside and out. They're just jealous."

Justina shook her head, unable to hide her disbelief. "Why would any of them be jealous of me?"

Michael bent his head to kiss her before answering. "Because you're a wonderful person, and they aren't. They don't know how to be real like you, so they try to bring you down to their level. When you fail to respond to their taunts in a satisfying manner, they just get worse."

Impressed, she nodded. "It's like you lived with them yourself."

Michael shook his head. "Fortunately, I've never endured it firsthand, but I've seen several patients at my counseling practice that lived through similar experiences. The important thing is that you don't let them change you, or make you unhappy."

She hugged him. "At this moment, I don't think I could be unhappy if I tried, Michael."

With impatience, they made it through the photo session, and then it was finally time for Elena to toss the bouquet before the newlyweds left for Vermont. By mutual agreement, she and Michael had set that as the point where they could officially retire to one of their rooms and spend the night in carnal bliss.

With some prodding from Elena and Michael, Justina joined the gaggle of single women waiting to catch the bouquet. Sasha was nearby, but she ignored her. She was annoyed to see Donella in the crowd, but her stepsister was an idiot. It wouldn't occur to her to sit out the bouquet toss since she was engaged.

Elena climbed onto a chair with Mitchell's assistance, her back to the women. "Ready, girls?"

Justina joined in with the rest to reply with an enthusiastic, "Yes."

"Here it comes." Elena covered her eyes with her free hand before tossing the bouquet dramatically. It sailed through the crowd, over the heads of the grasping girls, including Sasha and Donella. To Justina's surprise, the bouquet seemed to fall into her hands as if propelled by magic.

She looked up, finding Michael unerringly through the girls surrounding her with congratulations and hugs. There were a lot of details to work out yet, such as how they would build a relationship when he lived in Boston and she lived in New York, but her heart had her convinced they would figure it out.

Staring into Michael's eyes, the bride's words seemed prophetic to Justina when Elena shouted, "Justina's going to be the next one married."

Excerpt of "Desperate Measures"

FELICIA REENTERED HER office at Witherspoon's clutching a bag of Thai takeout from a nearby restaurant. A drizzling of rain had left her previously straightened hair a mass of kinky curls, and she ran a hand through it in an attempt to restore some semblance of order after setting lunch on her desk. It was hopeless, and she made a mental note to schedule a Brazilian blowout ASAP.

She took time to remove her raincoat, stow her purse in the bottom drawer of her desk and check the voicemail for messages before picking up the bag and moving to Clayton's office. A soft tap elicited an, "Enter," in his deep, New England baritone, and she opened the door.

Clayton looked up, his eyes gleaming darkly behind the silver frames of his reading glasses. The amber glow from the lamp on his desk brought out rich blue highlights in his black hair, making it difficult for Felicia to focus on the task he had set for her. She stood stupidly in the doorway, unable to tear her eyes from her boss.

A lock of hair flipped onto his forehead made her fingers itch to push it back, before proceeding down his face, to lightly caress the slight lines at his eyes. She would then move downward, across the strong bridge of his nose, to savor the firm texture of his full lips, before touching the slight cleft in his chin. Once her hands had explored the strong column of his throat, she would splay them across his chest as she sank onto his lap, her lips moist and ready to taste his....

Clayton clearing his throat brought her back to reality. With a shake of her head, Felicia did her best to hide her embarrassment at slipping into the fantasy. She lifted the bag higher. "Pad thai and green papaya salad, as requested."

He removed his glasses, setting them atop the file in one movement, even as he beckoned her forward with his other hand. Felicia's feet propelled her toward him, the heels of her shoes sinking into the frosted-gray carpet that was so plush it was probably more comfortable to sleep on than her own bed.

Upon reaching his desk, she put down the bag, opened it, and began removing the boxes. Each one was marked, so it was a simple matter to separate his order from hers. Silence filled the room while she completed the task, and Felicia tried to pretend she wasn't aware of Clayton's eyes sweeping over her as she worked. It was a difficult charade to maintain, since she could almost feel his sensual gaze touching her, caressing her intimately.

He wanted her as much as she wanted him. She was convinced they were both aware of the smoldering magnetism that arced between them whenever they shared the same space. Felicia knew enough about men to read the awareness in his eyes, to pick up on his subtle signals. She wasn't naïve enough to think Clayton lacked any experience with female companions, so she couldn't delude herself into thinking he didn't know she was equally attracted to him. The three months she had worked for him had only increased her attraction and, judging from recent behavior, his too.

Felicia's hands trembled slightly when she picked up the two boxes containing her order, along with a plastic fork, preparing to return to her desk. She held her breath, tensing as Clayton slid away from his desk to gain his feet. Her heart hammered in her ears when he walked toward her. She held breath escaped in a harsh exhalation when he brushed against her arm in the process of pointing to the cozy arrangement of a sofa, two chairs and a coffee table in the corner of his office.

"Stay, and have lunch with me."

Was she imagining the hint of smokiness in his tone? Felicia tried to appear nonchalant when she asked, "Shall I fetch the recorder?" The only times he had asked her to join him before had entailed working lunches, where he dictated memos into the recorder, or they discussed various strategies for dealing with a particular situation.

Clayton shook his head, scooped up his containers, and walked toward the sofa. His broad shoulders and lean waist, emphasized by the expertly tailored suit, drew her eyes, and it was all she could do not to fling herself at him.

With the fervent hope lunch was only foreplay, that finally some progress would take place today, leading them toward the seemingly inevitable affair, Felicia followed. Clayton had selected a middle cushion on the long sofa, and she sat beside him. The distance she left was enough to be provocative, but not completely blatant.

It took seconds to open her boxes, leaving her uncomfortably aware of his proximity and her lack of sparkling conversation. Being so close to him wasn't that unusual. After all, they worked together every day, usually in the confines of this office. But it was different today. Tension hung between them, and awareness of each other, of how easy it would be to lock the door and make love.

Or maybe she was imagining it all, Felicia wondered with a frown when Clayton leaned back and began eating. His posture suggested relaxation, without a hint of tension or suppressed awareness of her as more than his personal assistant. Had she manufactured in her own mind the exchanged glances that spoke of mutual longing? Was she so desperate for this man's touch that she was allowing herself to believe he was equally needy for hers?

Second-guessing her interpretation of his signals, Felicia absently picked at jasmine rice. As the silence stretched, her confidence grew shakier by the moment, until she was convinced she had imagined any sort of interest from her boss.

Panic took hold, and she buried the fork into the box and scooted away from him, ready to launch herself from the sofa and as far away from him as possible. Her face burned with humiliation, and she was desperate to escape. Silently, Felicia cursed Clayton when he finally decided to break the silence.

"What is it?" As he asked the question, Clayton grasped her forearm, his palm burning through the thin layer of silk separating them.

Felicia gasped when he rubbed a slow circle across her dark chocolate skin while turning her to face him. Her knees rested against his with the new position, and she had nowhere to look except into his eyes. They smoldered with banked desire. Her plump lips parted in response to his when she saw them forming a bow. Anticipation quickened her pulse and she arched forward, lifting her chin to facilitate the first meeting of their mouths.

She could already taste Clayton, had done so in countless nighttime fantasies, and it took every ounce of self-control to allow him to set the pace. He would appreciate that, since she suspected he enjoyed control in the bedroom as much as the boardroom.

His head lowered at a steady pace, and she waited impatiently. Her deep brown eyes closed when he got close enough for his breath to wash across her cheek. She curled her hands into fists in her lap to resist the urge to bury them into his hair and drag his mouth to hers.

Just as his lips were close enough for her to flick out her tongue to taste, the door opened without so much as a knock. A sound akin to a sob of frustration escaped Felicia, drowned out by the mechanical hum of George Witherspoon's wheelchair as it glided across the thick carpet.

His blue eyes raked over her, leaving Felicia exposed and raw, feeling as though he had measured her worth in a single glance and found her lacking. She leapt to her feet, counseling herself to act as though nothing unusual had been about to happen, even as she did her best to avoid the cold gaze of Clayton's father. "If you don't need me for anything else, Mr. Witherspoon, I'll leave you."

Clayton got to his feet slowly, his demeanor one of complete calm, as opposed to the one she feared she projected—guilt, though she had done nothing wrong. "That will be all, Ms. Calder."

She didn't miss the slight emphasis he placed on her surname. He seemed to want to remind her they had been on a first-name basis since her second week of employment. Was he exasperated by the way she had reacted to his father's unexpected entrance?

Felicia forced herself to walk steadily toward the door, holding her breath when she made it past George with little more than a sideways glance and dip of her head. Freedom from his contemptuous gaze was within sight when his voice froze her in place. "Just a moment, Miss Calder. I would like you to stay." Each word was issued coldly.

Somehow she swallowed the lump in her throat and managed a brittle smile when she turned to face George. Had she been braver, she would have pointed out she didn't answer to him, but all she managed was a limp, "Of course, sir."

It was as if he had read her unspoken thoughts. "How long have you been in my employ?"

"Three months."

George transferred his haughty gaze from her to his son. "You've lowered your standards, Clayton."

Felicia took a step back in reaction to the denouncement, even as Clayton moved toward his father, bridging the distance between them until he stood less than a foot behind her.

"You have no knowledge of what I look for in a personal assistant, nor of Felicia's qualifications, Father, so leave the hiring of my assistants to me," he said in a neutral tone, though his words had been a reproof of sorts. "Now, what brings you barging into my office?"

His father ignored the light reprimand and attempted turn of topic. "When I agreed to let you step in to my position, I expected you to maintain the company as I would have done. A pretty face is no excuse for a lapse in judgment."

Felicia gasped, but Clayton countered in a calm tone. "You hardly allowed me to take over willingly, Father." It was no secret George's stroke had left him incapacitated for months, forcing him to let his son finally have some real power in the company or risk losing everything to their competitors. She knew from Clayton—and from the old man's own behavior—that three years later, he was still bitter about no longer being in charge.

"That was a mistake that can be rectified. I'll remove you before you harm the company."

Clayton's cheeks flushed red, and a hint of annoyance appeared in his expression. She held her breath, wondering if she would witness an explosion of anger. Clayton had always been even-tempered and basically good-humored with her, but he had a reputation for being cold and calculating in business, with a hard edge reserved only for those who were dishonest in their dealings with the Witherspoon International.

His voice was soft, with only a subtle sibilance revealing the depths of his emotions. "Would you please leave us, Felicia?"

She might have remembered to nod as she scurried from the office, carefully avoiding George's eyes. Had the other man tried to call her back, she would have ignored his summons this time, having no desire to witness the argument between the two of them.

Out of habit, she closed the door behind her and went to her desk. Felicia sank into the chair, staring worriedly at the mahogany barrier separating her from Clayton and his father. In the three months she had worked for Clayton, twice before had she overheard him and his father arguing, both times via the phone, and had been privy only to Clayton's side.

Today was no different, except she could hear George's voice responding to his even tones. It carried over Clayton's, leaving no doubt to the extent of his rage. His pitch escalated with every exchange, until she could hear each syllable he spoke. If he hadn't been so enraged that he was speaking too rapidly for her to catch everything, she would have known exactly what he said.

Not that I need a transcript, she thought with a grimace. There was no mystery regarding the reason behind their exchange. Her. Clearly, the old man didn't approve of her, but Clayton was refusing to kowtow to his demands to get rid of her. At least Felicia hoped she was correctly interpreting the argument. Was it silly to have so much faith in him, to believe so firmly he would defend her to his father?

The office door opening, followed by George's chair whirring through it, broke her musings. She looked up, flinching at the derogatory glare the old man shot her way. Hands clutched in her lap, she stared at him without speaking as he negotiated his way toward the door that would lead him from their office suite to the main hall. She held her breath as he neared the door, daring to hope she would escape any further exchanges with him.

At the doorway, his glower deepened. "Don't get too comfortable behind that desk, Miss Calder."

When he was gone, she breathed a sigh of relief. It was difficult to take his parting words seriously when she knew Clayton must have refused to dismiss her. After her last disaster of a job, she couldn't stand the thought of being fired and forced to seek new employment with an even larger gap in her work history.

That, and she didn't want to leave so abruptly without finding out how things would turn out between herself and Clayton. Felicia groaned at the small voice that insisted on pointing out such thoughts. She schooled her expression into one of professional detachment when Clayton entered her office.

The tense arrangement of his features suggested he still bore anger from the exchange with his father, but he sounded as calm as ever when he spoke. "As soon as you've finished lunch, I'd like the Sterling file on my desk."

"Right away." Felicia managed a weak smile. "I've lost my appetite."

He nodded, his expression softening slightly. "As have I." With a single nod, he returned to his office.

She watched him go, attempting to suppress her disappointment. They had been so close to acting on their attraction. If not for George's intervention, they might be entangled in a passionate embrace this very second.

A long sigh escaped her when she left her desk to fetch the requested file. Maybe it was for the best. She knew firsthand how difficult it could be to work alongside someone whose attraction was out in the open. She didn't need that kind of scenario again. Yes, she had learned her lesson about office relationships working with Marco Trivanni.

That treacherous voice in the back of her mind insisted on tormenting her again by posing a question she was unable to banish from her mind for the rest of the afternoon. If she really intended to avoid an affair with Clayton, why was she still imagining what it would be like to make love with her boss?

FELICIA HADN'T REALIZED how on-edge she had been until she left Witherspoon's later that afternoon. As soon as her sensible sedan cleared the underground parking garage, she exhaled and her stiff shoulders relaxed. The events of the afternoon had cast a pall over both of them. She just hadn't allowed herself to acknowledge the new level of tension between her and Clayton until safely away from his presence.

She pointed her car in the direction of her sister's dorm, though all she really wanted to do was go home to a hot bath and try to pretend the day hadn't turned out as it had. She didn't want to feel uncomfortable around Clayton, but he had seemed to avoid her for the remainder of the afternoon. If she had to identify the reason, she might have tentatively settled on embarrassment from George's behavior, but that wasn't quite right. Had she imagined the flashes of guilt she seemed to read in his expression the few times work had necessitated they interact?

As she approached the two-story building one block from Tanja's college campus, Felicia tried to force the thoughts from her mind. Her distress would transmit easily to her sister, and she didn't need to pick up on her negative emotions. Tanja needed positive support for the forthcoming doctor's appointment.

Tanja was waiting for her at the entrance to the building, conversing with a fellow student. He was a handsome young man, with sunglasses that gave his face a lean, sexy look.

Felicia honked twice, and Tanja waved in her direction. She held her breath as her little sister negotiated the stairs with careless confidence. It took every fiber in her being not to get out and guide her sister to the car as Tanja tapped out the path with the white cane in her hands. Though she had only been using the cane for a few months, it seemed a natural extension of her body. Felicia wished she had adapted as well to the quick deterioration of her sister's eyesight as Tanja had. It was still in her to protect her from everything that could pose a danger, but her sister preferred to do things on her own.

Once she was settled into the passenger seat and safely belted in, Felicia let out the breath she had been holding, greeted her sister, and turned the car in the direction of Tanja's ophthalmologist. As she drove the few blocks to his office, they chatted about Tanja's latest class.

Felicia was thankful she didn't ask about work since Tanja had an uncanny knack to pick up on the slightest change in tone. Her sister loved to tease her about her "crush" on Clayton, and Felicia was in no mood to evade or deny the teasing allegations today. Nor did she want to relate what had happened with George, knowing it would outrage her little sister. She needed to keep her stress levels down.

Parking was tight, but Felicia angled into a spot on the street. She bit her tongue to avoid uttering a protest when Tanja bounded from the car before she had even finished parallel parking.

"I'll see you in there."

"Okay." Felicia waited until Tanja cleared the curb before angling her car the rest of the way into the space. She might have watched her sister until she made it inside the office if not for an impatient honk behind her. As she turned off the ignition, her cell phone beeped to alert her to an incoming text message.

After assuring herself Tanja had made it inside, Felicia retrieved the phone from the pocket on her purse and flipped it open. In two seconds, she had the message on her screen.

Felicia, come in ASAP. Major crisis with Sterling merger.

Experiencing a twinge of guilt, Felicia closed the phone without answering Clayton's summons. It was clear he needed her, but Tanja needed her more right then.

By the time she entered the ophthalmologist's office, Tanja was already on her way back. Felicia slipped in behind her sister and the nurse. As they went into the back office, she winced at the sight of a new painting hanging on the wall. Tanja would have loved the pixilated painting of a floral arrangement partially obscuring a Victorian maiden, if only she could have seen it.

Felicia tried to cling to hope as they were ushered into an exam room. Maybe her sister would one day see again and be able to have a normal life, to finish her studies in art history and re-enroll in a regular university, instead of the one she currently attended, tailored for the needs of the blind and visually impaired.

Dr. Batts's arrival interrupted her private thoughts, and she managed a smile for the middle-aged man. He took time to shake both their hands and exchange small talk before performing a brief exam on Tanja. Felicia held her breath when he sat down on a stool and opened the file on the counter.

"Last week's test results are back. Nothing's changed, Tanja." He sounded genuinely regretful. "The vision in your right eye remains at 20/400 and 20/600 in your left."

"So, no further degeneration then?" Tanja asked with false cheer.

Felicia easily detected the disappointment in her sister's airy tone. "But no improvement."

"There wouldn't be, Ms. Calder. As I've explained, Retinitis Pigmentosa doesn't spontaneously regress. All we can hope to do is halt the progress of the degeneration of the retina." Dr. Batts shook his bald head. "There isn't a cure."

"There must be something you can do. Tanja is young. Her vision has only been affected for the last year or so."

"She's only noticed symptoms for the past year. The RP has been destroying her retinal cells since the day she was born." A sigh escaped the ophthalmologist. "The only possible cure remains the procedure I've discussed with you before, and the odds aren't that favorable."

Felicia nodded, feeling a familiar sense of defeat crushing her. The cost of enrolling Tanja in the clinical trial through a private facility in Boston was astronomical. Even if they could somehow convince the clinic to take Tanja without cost, her sister would still need full living expenses and medical assistance during the months of treatment. She just couldn't afford it.

She tuned out the doctor as he and Tanja wrapped up the appointment. It took every ounce of willpower not to cry when she walked beside her sister a few minutes later, subtly guiding her to the car.

"I feel like pizza," said Tanja as she slipped into the car. Her hand unerringly found the seat belt, and she seemed to function as well without her sight as she had with it, but Felicia knew the toll it had taken on her to lose her sight so rapidly.

"Sorry, kiddo, but I have to go back to the office. You can order in, can't you?"

Tanja frowned at her when she had settled behind the steering wheel. "You work too much, sis." She shrugged. "Well, next time. You can drop me at Mario's on your way back to Witherspoon's."

"That's so far from your dorm."

"Six blocks. I think I can cover that distance without dropping from exhaustion." The dry note in her voice did little to cover the exasperation Tanja was trying to mask.

"What if you get lost?"

"I won't."

"You could be injured—"

"Enough," she said sharply. "God, Felicia, you're my sister, not my keeper. I'll be fine."

Felicia bit her tongue, managing a tight, "Okay." She understood Tanja's need for independence, but couldn't stop worrying about her. It had become habit to take care of her sister since their parents died, and having her sister go blind in the span of a year didn't make it easier to let go of her responsibilities.

Tanja didn't speak again until she pulled up in front of the kitschy pizza parlor. Her tone was light and mellow, the same as always. "Thanks for the ride."

She struggled to match it. "Sure." A husky note entered her voice. "Take care."

"I will." Unexpectedly, Tanja leaned over to press a kiss on her cheek. "You take care as well."

"I don't think dealing with merger issues will endanger me."

"But resisting your boss's charms might." With a giggle, Tanja made her escape from the car before Felicia could respond.

She accomplished the drive back to the office in good time. Her mind continued to worry at how to get Tanja into the trial, but she forced herself to focus on the Sterling merger and everything about it she could recall while swiping her card to enter the building. The elevator ferried her to the top floor quickly, and by the time she stepped out, she had on a professional face.

As she walked down the marble hallway, the clicking of her heels echoing to remind her she was practically alone in the building, Felicia wondered if she had been summoned into the office for something other than the Sterling merger. Was Clayton about to make a move? Her stomach churned with a mix of apprehension and excitement when she walked into the office.

It was immediately clear she had been called under false pretenses, but not for the passionate reason she'd hoped. George was an imposing figure, even in the wheelchair, framed as he was by the late afternoon light spilling in through the office's sole window. "Miss Calder."

She frowned. "What's going on? Why are you here?"

"I'm here to get rid of a problem—you."

Excerpt of "Cynthia And The Prince"

MAYBE THAT CONFIDENCE had come too soon. She was forced to consider the idea as she gazed around her when stepping foot into the summer palace of the royal family, where they were currently in residence. It was luxurious beyond compare, and enough to really underscore to her how out-of-place she was with her Midwestern, middleclass upbringing when contrasted with her surroundings.

Firming her shoulders, she reminded herself she was there for her expertise in physical therapy, and because she wasn't afraid of a challenge. This might be outside her comfort zone, but she couldn't let that hold her back.

By the time she recognized a familiar face a few moments later, she was feeling more certain again. She walked forward to meet Shawn, who was beaming at her. His dark skin had gotten a couple of shades darker, and his curls, neatly cropped close to his head last time she'd seen him, had grown out into a two-inch high start of an Afro. He looked tired, but also fantastic.

The abrasive sound of a throat clearing broke apart their hug of greeting, and she smoothed down her slacks and shirt before turning to face the source. Somehow, she kept a pleasant smile on her lips even as she faced the expression of disapproval directed her way. The owner of the expression was a tall, sour-looking brunette with a furrow in her brow that looked like it was there perpetually. Right away, she was certain it was the Lisandra Montagne Shawn had mentioned to her.

"Now that you're here, I'll show you to the servants' quarters. The driver will have already sent in your bags. After that, the doctor will want you to meet the prince, I'm sure. Once that's finished, I have a list of rules to discuss with you."

Cynthia firmed her spine and took a step closer. She extended her hand as she said, "Hello. You must be Ms. Montagne. Thank you for making the travel arrangements." For a moment, her hand remained there with no sign of acknowledgement.

Eventually, Lisandra made a production of juggling the items in her hands to take her hand in a limp-fish squeeze before quickly releasing it. "Of course, Ms. Hillsboro. It's my job to help the royal family, and the doctor seems to think you might provide some assistance to Prince Logan."

There was a chill in the air, and Cynthia briefly wondered if Shawn and Lisandra had a thing—or had once had a thing, and the woman was jealous of the history between them. Once the other woman cast a frigid, dismissive glance at Shawn, she quickly revised that hypothesis. Whatever Lisandra's problem, it wasn't because she was involved with Shawn, or because Cynthia had once dated him.

It didn't take long for Lisandra to show her to a room three floors up. It was toward the back of the palatial home, and when she left her at the door, she parted with a crisp, "Next time you enter, please use the servants' entrance instead of the main entryway, Ms. Hillsboro."

Before Cynthia could acknowledge the admonishment, or even think about telling her the driver had dropped her at the main entrance, the other woman was gone in a cloud of expensive perfume and surrounded by an invisible, impenetrable icy shield. With a shrug, she watched her leave before entering her room.

It wasn't as opulent as everything else she'd seen, but it was a room reserved for servants. Everything was rather spartan, but all clean and of obviously excellent quality. She was certain the bedframe, though plain, was an antique by the patina on the wood. The armoire and dresser were the same. There was nothing about which to complain—not that she would have anyway. It would have started off her employment on the wrong foot, and she was certain Lisandra wouldn't have cared if she was sleeping on a bed of nails. She gave off that kind of vibe.

It had been a long flight, though hardly a burden on the private jet they had arranged for her. She'd felt almost guilty wasting all those resources for just herself, but hadn't exactly minded having the whole space to herself without having to share idle conversation with strangers. Still, she hadn't been able to sleep no matter how she'd tried, and she was starting to feel the effects of not sleeping for almost ten hours.

She pushed aside her exhaustion, going into the bathroom that appeared to connect to another door that was currently unlocked, and splashed water on her face. Her makeup was nonexistent by that point, but she didn't bother adding more. It was too much effort. The curls in her shoulder-length hair were frizzy, but she didn't bother to smooth them or add product.

When she stepped out of her room a few minutes later, she was unsurprised to find Shawn waiting for her. She smiled at him and wove her arm through his, allowing him to take a bit of her weight as he led her down the hallway.

"Icy Lisandra put you in the middle of nowhere, didn't she?"

She shrugged. "I don't know. Probably. Where are you?"

"I'm in a room next to Logan's, in his wing of the house, but Icy Lisandra hates that. She likes to remind me every chance she gets that I'm an employee, not a guest, and certainly not worthy of a suite." He laughed.

"She's as charming as I expected."

He shrugged. "Let's see if I did Logan justice in describing him."

Cynthia swallowed down a bit of nervousness. "Yeah, okay." By the time they made the long trek to the prince's wing, she'd had plenty of time to quell her nerves.

They still flared to life again when Shawn knocked on one of two French doors before entering. She followed him inside, looking around surreptitiously and trying not to ogle the blatant display of wealth.

"Logan, where are you, man?" asked Shawn.

"In here," called a deep voice with a crisp accent. It wasn't quite English-sounding, but similar.

From the research she'd done before coming to Arganeaux, she knew the small island country had been founded when Mad George the Third banished his ill-liked distant relation there and ordered him imprisoned. At some point, the imprisonment had turned to a governorship during the Regent's reign, and Arganeaux had been an independent monarchy for the last hundred-plus years after a brief, nearly bloodless war with England. Their rich oil deposits and rare Earth minerals probably had something to do with England's acquiescence.

She held her breath as the prince came into sight, battling the latest surge of nerves. Her first sight of him wasn't the professional evaluation it should be. Instead, she noticed his lean, toned physique displayed by the tight white tank top he wore. It wasn't what she would've expected from a Prince, but she couldn't argue that it certainly highlighted how muscular his arms were—which reminded her that she was there to work, not ogle the prince.

This time, when she ran her gaze down his body, it was more professional as she assessed his strengths. It was good that he had strong arms, because he needed them to lift himself in and out of the chair and to be able to move it on his own. She was pleased to see it was a manual wheelchair, instead of a power chair, which would have reduced his need to exercise and might have made his recovery that much slower. Either Shawn or one of the physical therapists must have been responsible for that choice, because she doubted the hospital and convalescent homes where he had spent his first few weeks would have tried to persuade him to go with the manual chair if he'd insisted on a power one.

Summoning a deep breath and a smile, she moved her gaze from his body to his face, muscles immediately tightening at the smug expression he wore. Her smile felt strained under the prince's gaze. She caught her breath slightly at the odd coloring, somewhere between purple and blue, and fringed by long brown eyelashes. His face was symmetrical perfection, as though carved by a skilled sculptor, and his cheekbones looked sharp enough to cut any finger that dared wander down it. She might've been overwhelmed by his appearance if not for the faint curl of his lips and the complete disinterest in his gaze.

Shawn stepped forward, putting a casual hand on her midback as he urged her forward. "This is the new physical therapist I told you about, Logan. Cynthia Hillsboro, meet Prince Logan Arbonnaire."

She held out her hand, realizing after extending it that he had no intention of reciprocating. She let it hang awkwardly for a moment before dropping it back to her side. She was still nervous, but was quickly becoming familiar with another emotion—annoyance.

"You did that wrong, Shawn. You're supposed to introduce the prince to the commoner first, not the other way around." His voice was a rich baritone, and his accent was not quite English, but even more alluring in its uniqueness. It was too bad he apparently only used it to deliver scathing comments.

Shawn shrugged. "Royal decorum isn't my thing, Logan."

The prince didn't reply to Shawn's comment. Instead, his gaze hardened as he looked up at Cynthia after letting his gaze sweep over her form in a similar fashion to the one she'd used to appraise him. When he met her eyes, he gave her a lazy smile. "You're younger than I expected, and prettier too. You should consider makeup and doing something with your hair."

She squeezed her hands into fists as she took a deep breath while reminding herself this might be the prince's coping mechanism. Even if it wasn't, and she had to deal with that sort of attitude every day, she could do it. She'd had difficult patients before, and she had come expecting an adversarial relationship with the prince, at least in the beginning. "You aren't what I expected either, Your Highness."

He cocked a brow. "How so?"

She just shrugged, not wanting to get into a discussion of the importance of manners. "If you're ready, I'd like to do an assessment."

He stiffened slightly. "What does that entail?"

She arched a brow. "Did neither one of your previous physical therapists ask for an assessment?"

His expression darkened. "The hideous dragon lady from Belgium attempted such a thing, but I refused to cooperate. The simpering miss from Filoni seemed to use it as an excuse to fondle the royal prince."

She resisted the urge to loudly assure him she wouldn't do such a thing. Instead, she managed a smile and asked sweetly, "Would you please consent, Prince Logan? I need to know where you are, so I can figure out the best way to help you reach your maximum potential."

He stiffened again, his expression completely closed off. "There's nothing you can do to help me."

"Won't you at least give me a chance to try?" She squared her shoulders. "I'm very good at what I do."

He made a scoffing sound. "How old are you? You look like you've barely finished college."

"I'm twenty-seven," she said in an even tone. "I'm a fully qualified physical therapist, and I've helped a lot of clients. Even those who don't want to be helped, and who were very stubborn about the whole situation." She bit her tongue as she uttered the indiscreet words, but couldn't call them back.

He glared up at her. "I don't like your tone, or your attitude. Send her home, Shawn."

"No," said Shawn and Cynthia simultaneously.

She took a step closer to the prince before kneeling down to be closer to his level. She kept her tone brisk. "You need help, and I'm not going anywhere."

"You're fired, and I'll fire him too if you don't get out."

Shawn seemed unconcerned with the threat as he crouched down on the other side of the prince's chair. "I've already spoken with the king, and he assures me that my job is secure, as is Cynthia's, unless she does something grossly incompetent. We all want to help you, and you know that, Logan."

Logan glared at him before turning his heated gaze on Cynthia. "It appears I'm stuck with you."

She nodded just once. "Yes, it does. Now, should we do the assessment?"

He didn't resist, but his lack of participation was obvious over the next twenty minutes as she evaluated his form and remaining function. It was an emotionally exhausting experience, and one of the worst sessions she had ever done, and they hadn't even started the difficult things yet. It was a relief when he pulled his chair back a few feet, rolling backward, and crossed his arms over his chest.

"I'm done being your damn guinea pig for today Ms. Hillsboro. Get out of my room now."

She could have argued and insisted on continuing, but there was no need. She had enough basic information to put together a treatment plan, and she wanted to escape the prince's constant presence for a while as she recomposed herself. Without another word to him or Shawn, she turned and left.

She drew up short a few feet down the corridor when she ran into Lisandra Montagne, who was clearly waiting for her. She bit back a groan and attempted a small smile. "I'd almost forgotten you had something you wanted to discuss with me."

"We'll talk while we walk back to your quarters." She left no choice but to follow as she turned and started walking briskly down the hallway.

Cynthia fell into step behind her, vaguely aware of Shawn catching up with them as they moved down the corridor.

"Take this." As she spoke, Lisandra pivoted slightly to drop a thick booklet into Cynthia's hand. Her brisk steps never faltered. "Take time to memorize it."

"What is it?" As she asked the question, she glanced down at the title and frowned. "Employee handbook." Was she an employee, or was she an independent consultant?

"As I said, read it and memorize it. There are certain rules and standards to which you must adhere. You have to learn protocol and decorum, and what is acceptable behavior." Lisandra stopped and spun around, glaring at Shawn for a moment before her gaze cooled as it moved to Cynthia's. "You're here as an employee, not a friend. It would be wise to remember that and behave accordingly."

"Lisandra certainly hates it when us commoners dare become friends with the royalty," said Shawn with a chuckle, clearly unconcerned by Lisandra's opinion on the matter.

The brunette glared daggers at him again. "It would behoove some to learn their place."

Shawn didn't bother with a response as he turned to face Cynthia with a grin. "Don't be too afraid of her. She's King Harrison's right-hand man, but she doesn't wield half the power that she thinks she does."

Lisandra sniffed at him. She also seemed to choose to ignore his reply as she focused on Cynthia. "The prince needs a physical therapist, not another friend. Remember that, and you'll do well here."

Cynthia somehow stifled the urge to roll her eyes. "I'm here to help the prince, and I can't imagine ever becoming friends with him. He's too unpleasant."

Lisandra looked scandalized. "Please refer immediately to your manual, chapter four subsection seventeen-A. You'll see you're not allowed to say such things."

Cynthia couldn't hold back the eye roll that time despite her best efforts. "I'll certainly look through the manual and try to devote some attention to decorum in between focusing on helping the prince reach his full potential again. Thank you for your time, Ms. Montagne." It was a dismissal, and she was able to pull it off because they had returned to the room she'd been assigned earlier. She swept past the king's assistant, nodded to Shawn on the way, and closed the door behind her.

As soon as the door was settled in the jamb, she leaned back against it and took a deep breath. Her heart was pounding, and she was gripped by myriad emotions. She didn't know whether she wanted to laugh, cry, or scream.

Briefly, she wondered if she had made the wrong choice by coming to Arganeaux. Shawn had warned her it would be difficult, and she'd thought she had prepared herself, but it seemed obvious that it was going to be the hardest assignment she'd ever undertaken. The sense of excitement she'd experienced in the face of a new challenge before failed to rise this time, and she let out a deep breath as she stood up and moved away from the door, dropping the manual provided by Lisandra on a writing table nearby as she did so.

About Mylia

IF YOU WOULD LIKE TO be the first to hear about new releases, please join my mailing list[1] and receive a free book. I love to hear from readers, so please feel free to email me at authormashton@yahoo.com.

---

1. https://subscribeto.eo.page/myliaashton

Did you love *Vegas Mistake*? Then you should read *Inferno* by Mylia Ashton!

Sparks fly when Nico Martin rescues Elysia Walsh from a fire at her clinic. She has a predictable routine to which she clings. Nico is impulsive and the complete antithesis of her. There's no denying the attraction between them, but when she's determined to avoid commitment, and he's falling fast, their fling could go up in flames.

Also by Mylia Ashton

The Brotherhood
Saved By The Master Sergeant
Sheltered By The Sergeant Major

Standalone
Vegas Mistake
Marooned With The Billionaire Doctor
Enemies To Expecting
Cynthia And The Prince
Desperate Measures
Inferno